D1165907

Carlson, Dale Bick.
    The frog people / by Dale Carlson ;
with drawings by Michael Garland. --
1st ed. -- New York : E.P. Dutton,
c1982.
    75 p. : ill. ; 22 cm. -- (A Skinny
book)

    ISBN 0-525-45107-2

    I. Garland, Michael, ill.   II.
Title.

The Frog People

by Dale Carlson

with drawings by Michael Garland

A SKINNY BOOK

E. P. Dutton   New York

Library of Congress Cataloging in Publication Data

Carlson, Dale Bick.   The frog people.
(A Skinny book)

Summary: A young woman frantically searches for a
way to prevent any more residents of Proud Point
from being transformed into frogs.
[1. Science fiction]
I. Garland, Michael, ill.   II. Title.
PZ7.C21645Fs   1982   [Fic]   81-12659
ISBN 0-525-45107-2   AACR2

Published in the United States by E. P. Dutton, Inc.,
2 Park Avenue, New York, N.Y. 10016

Published simultaneously in Canada by Clarke,
Irwin & Company Limited, Toronto and Vancouver

Editor: Ann Durell   Designer: Isabel Warren-Lynch

Printed in the U.S.A.   First Edition
10 9 8 7 6 5 4 3 2 1

this book with my heart
for the real Dan Fitzgibbon
the most wonderful miracle of all

1

The fog came. The tides rolled back. And the terrible things washed up out of the sea. Ann Derry was the first to see them.

Ann walked on the shore every morning. It was a good place to think. And she loved the white lighthouse out on the sea. But this spring morning it was cold.

Ann sat on a dune. The wind was less sharp here. She let sand fall through her hands. This was where she came when she wanted to get away from Proud Point. This was where she came when she wanted to be alone.

Ann could see Proud Point. It was half a mile

1

up the beach. Less than two hundred people in that old fishing town. Old families in that old town. Old busy-bodies too. In Proud Point, if you needed to think, you took to the sea. Or you took a walk. Or, like Ann and Daniel Fitzgibbon, you ran.

Ann had run her five miles that morning. Dan, stronger and faster, was still doing his ten.

Ann waited on the dunes for Dan as always. As always, they would drive to school together. Dan was an English teacher and sports coach at Central High School. Ann taught natural science.

Proud Point was a peaceful place. Until that morning, they had all lived a peaceful life.

Ann looked up toward town. What was on the beach? There seemed to be one large thing and a lot of small things. Ann stood up and began walking toward them. She felt her spine shiver. It was the shiver she felt in the wild when there was danger.

"You're going to be a *what*?" Uncle Charles had said. It was five years ago that Ann had told him her plan.

"An ethologist," said Ann. "A person who learns about animals in their own places."

"But that can be dangerous," said Uncle Charles. "I don't like to think of you in the middle of a jungle."

Ann's parents had died when she was a little girl. Uncle Charles had taken her to live with him in his big old house near the sea.

"You are the Dr. Charles Proud who takes care of people," Ann had said. "I am going to be the Dr. Ann Derry who understands animals."

"You always did like animals better than people," Uncle Charles said. "All right. But please, no jungles for a while."

So when Ann got her degree, she got a grant to study a group of animals near Proud Point. She didn't mind a bit. She loved Uncle Charles. She loved Proud Point. Most of all, she loved Dan Fitzgibbon.

Thinking about him, she began to smile.

Then she stopped smiling. The shiver inside her was stronger.

She was nearer those things on the beach now. They were only a few yards away.

The first shock was bad enough. She saw that what the sea had washed up was the body of a man. Ann couldn't see his face. It was in the sand. Near him lay smaller things. They were the bodies, pale and dead, of tiny green frogs.

On the beach, the wind stirred the sand. Ann drew closer and brushed it off the still body at her feet. She felt the shivering inside her turn into a deep chill. As a scientist, she was used to death. But there was something more here. Ann knew this, even before she rolled the man's body face up to the sky.

The second shock was a horror she could not believe.

2

The face of the dead man was green. It was the same green as the dead frogs. The eyes were the same too. They were big, open. They seemed to pop in terror. And his mouth was a wide slit, like a frog's mouth. It grinned horribly up at her.

Ann froze. But she was a scientist. Her training made her look carefully. She knew these young frogs could only have come from a pond in the woods several miles inland. She also saw that their death was not from natural causes. It was from surgery. Ann would need to look at them in a lab to find out what parts had been removed.

Poor, sad frogs.

"Now the man," Ann ordered herself.

The dead, green skin, the open, popping eyes, the wide frog mouth made Ann feel sick. The head, as flat as a frog's, was as green and hairless as the face. The hands, Ann noted, were webbed, with skin between the fingers.

It was clear that the man had been killed. Maybe there were signs of surgery, some terrible experimenting. If what Ann guessed about the man's death were true, she would need some help. She would need Dan on her side. Proud Point people were born with cricks in their necks, for looking the other way from trouble.

So Ann decided to find Dan.

She ran across the dunes to the path above the rocks.

She stayed on the path around the cove, past the dock, past the fishing boats, past the crying gulls.

As she ran up Center Street, no one stopped her. Proud Point was used to runners now.

"When's Daniel's next marathon?" called out old Jane Marsh. She sat on the porch of her country store. She had sat there for fifty years. She had watched Ann and Dan grow up together.

"Not until spring," Ann called back over her shoulder.

She passed Hart's Book Store. The three Harts would be out running.

"Hear your study grant came through," said John Ward. He owned the bank. "Good for you."

"Thanks," Ann called back.

"Yes, good for you," another voice called after her.

This was George Granger. George owned Blackstone. Blackstone was Proud Point's guest house. It was a big, dark house on the sea, a jumble of roofs and pointed towers. Ann could see it as she ran. It was beyond the town, across the salt marshes.

George took in everything at Blackstone. Stray cats and dogs, lost baby skunks, or human guests were all one to George. He had even taken in Uncle Charles's friend, Dr. Emil Storm. He let Dr. Storm use Blackstone's cellars for a lab. Ann liked George for taking in the old scientist. But she couldn't stop to talk now.

On she ran. It was on the track near Pine Pond that she found Dan. That was the pond of the tiny green frogs. She told Dan her story as calmly as she could.

9

"But if I tell you about the man, you won't believe me," said Ann. "Something awful was done to him before he died. Something to do with the frogs. Please come with me now."

"You reported this to Cliff on your way to find me, right?" said Dan. Cliff Kirkland was Dan's best friend and Proud Point's sheriff.

"No. I want you to see the body first. Also, I want to look at the frogs again before they're taken away," said Ann.

Dan's arm went around her.

"Honey, we still have to report this to the sheriff," he said. "Tell you what. I'll shoot past school, let them know we'll be late. Then I'll get Cliff from the sheriff's office. You just go on down to the beach and wait for us."

Ann looked up at him.

"I'm glad you're not just good-looking," said Ann. "I'm glad you understand things."

Dan brought Cliff Kirkland, the sheriff, and his deputy, Susan Whelan, to the beach.

Ann Derry was there.

Only the body was not.

10

3

Ann smiled sweetly.

"So good of you to come," she said.

"Why does she sound like this is a tea party?" said Cliff. "Dan, you said she found a body. And a lot of dead frogs." Cliff's dark eyes looked up and down the beach. "Susan, my pet, do you see anything?"

Susan looked up and down the beach. "You don't think these two are playing a joke on us again, Cliff, do you? It wouldn't be the first time. You remember the ice in our beds after the Boston run?"

Susan and Cliff looked at Dan Fitzgibbon.

Dan Fitzgibbon looked at Ann Derry.

Ann Derry kept on smiling.

She didn't look exactly at anybody.

"Don't say anything now," said Cliff. "I might put both of you behind bars for waking me up. Just talk it over. And tell me a good story later."

"You can tell me a good story now," said Dan, when Susan and Cliff had left.

"Okay," said Ann. "But just remember how understanding you are."

She walked fifty yards down the beach to the rocks. Dan followed. On the other side of the rocks was the dead body. Near the body were the dead frogs. Ann had pulled the body there. She had covered it with beach brush and wood.

"Please, Dan, I mean it. I really want you to see these first. And I really do want to do a lab exam before Cliff takes them away. I just need tonight, okay?"

"What do you mean, tonight?" said Dan.

"We can't be seen doing what we're going to do," said Ann.

"Which means we're going to do something wrong, right? We're going to take a body that doesn't belong to us, keep a body that doesn't

13

belong to us, lie about a body that doesn't belong to us—" Dan stopped.

Ann was smiling again, her sweet smile.

So Dan stopped. He even grinned back.

"All right," he said. "But just until tonight."

The gulls were crying when they met on the beach that evening.

Ann pulled off the beach brush so Dan could see. The horror of the dead man's face was even more freakish by moonlight. The green skin, the popping eyes, the wide, frog-like mouth made Ann feel as bad as before.

"Have you examined the rest of the body?" Dan asked. He held the flat, hairless green head.

"Only some of it. I didn't want to be seen out here."

"What have you found so far?" Dan asked.

"The feet and the hands are webbed," Ann answered. "The skin is frog-like—green, soft, damp. The tongue, like that of any frog, is long and sticky." Ann spoke the words quickly over the poor thing on the sand. It was that or cry.

"What do you mean, *any* frog?" asked Dan.

"Just that," Ann answered. "This man has become like the most common frog in North

America. The kind you see in any river or pond in any woods. The kind I've seen Dr. Emil Storm getting near Pine Pond for some work he says he's doing."

"What do you mean, *says* he's doing?" said Dan.

"Just that," said Ann. Her mouth was firm.

Dan's gentle hands rested the webbed hand on the sand. He stood up, reading Ann like a book.

"Meaning," he said, "you want to go across those salt marshes to Blackstone and sneak down to Dr. Storm's lab."

"Yes," nodded Ann. "But not just me, darling."

"I will not carry a dead frog man and a lot of dead frogs all the way from here to Blackstone," said Dan.

"No, of course not," said Ann. "I'll carry the frogs."

"Thanks," said Dan.

"And," said Ann, "Dr. Storm will be asleep by the time we get there. He never locks up. So I can use the lab to do some tests on the bodies. And also see just what Dr. Storm is up to."

She helped lift the body to Dan's back. Then she picked up the frogs and put them in a large bag.

15

They could see Blackstone's roofs and towers against the dark night sky.

Ann shivered. She was seldom afraid. She was afraid now.

4

Down the dark stairs they went. Ann led the way into the lab. She lighted one light. It cast shadows over the big water tanks around the room. Dr. Storm was an aquabiologist. He studied life that lived in fresh water. The light also showed two lab tables with test tubes, burners, and all the rest of Dr. Storm's things.

Dan put the body on a table. Ann put the frogs nearby. Then the two of them moved toward a huge tank in the middle of the lab and stared.

In the tank was a horror show.

"Horrible even for a scientist," muttered Ann.

There were parts of frogs: legs, heads, middle parts, eyes. There were parts of humans: legs, heads, middles, eyes. And there were parts that were both frog and human together: human legs with frog feet, frog heads with human eyes.

"How has he made these horrors?" asked Dan.

"I don't know yet," said Ann.

Ann pinned down three frogs under a strong light. The frogs had each been slit open carefully by a doctor who knew what he was doing. Ann examined the frogs.

"Their livers are missing," said Ann.

"What does that mean?" Dan asked.

"I wish I knew," said Ann. "The liver is the largest gland in the body. It causes important changes in the blood. It also helps us to break down and change the food we eat."

She went over to stare at the poor dead body on the table.

"This man wasn't changed by surgery. My guess is that the frogs' livers were used in some kind of formula. The formula was given to this man."

Ann turned and pointed to the tank. "The same formula was given to the parts of frogs and human beings in there. And it made the changes we see."

While Ann talked, Dan had been looking closely at the body under a strong light.

"There aren't any needle marks that I can find," said Dan. "But have a look at these."

Ann bent over. There, on the soft, damp, green skin of the man's back, were two ugly dark spots. They were like bad burns.

Dan spoke slowly. "I've read about poisons that can just be put on the skin with a piece of cloth or cotton. The poison burns its way in slowly. Suppose the frog formula works like one of those poisons."

Ann worked for two hours. Dan took notes for her. They decided not to face Dr. Storm tonight. First they would get everything to a safe place.

It was four in the morning when they finished. The body and the frogs were in the room behind Cliff's office. Ann hid the slides and test tubes in the lab at the high school.

At five, when the sky began to grow light before sunrise, they were in the Proud house.

"Coffee?" asked Dan.

"You said it!" Ann almost ran for the kitchen.

Before she got there, a knock came from the front door. Ann went and opened it.

There was old Jane Marsh, holding the hand

of small Jane, her granddaughter. Ann held out her arms to the scared child and looked up at Dan.

Even in the dim hall light, they could both see it.

The child's eyes were pushing out. And her skin was frog green.

5

"I woke up," said small Jane. "When I looked in the mirror, I got scared. What's the matter with me, Ann?"

"We'll get Dr. Proud out of bed," said Ann. "He'll help you feel better."

She and Dan looked at each other. They were both thinking of the dead body. There was no more time for secrets. There was a child involved now.

"I'll get Cliff and Susan," said Dan.

"I'll get some coffee going," said old Jane. "Dan, why not get your brother Jake down from the farm? He's got a good head in bad times."

Dan nodded. Jake had taken over the farm and had raised Dan after their parents had died. Dan had moved to town. But Jake kept to himself on the farm not far from Pine Pond. Jake was someone both Ann and Dan trusted.

"I'm coming with you," said Ann. "And we'll bring John Ward and George Granger back too."

Small Jane's eyes seemed to grow larger. Her mouth was a slit grinning up at Ann. "Is everybody coming to see me?" she said, pleased.

"Yes, sweetheart," said Ann.

"What about Dr. Storm?" said Dan.

"Maybe not yet?" Ann said quietly.

Dan answered her silent question. "Maybe not yet," he agreed.

Ann led the child upstairs and left her with Uncle Charles.

Dan had the car waiting when she came back down. They picked up Cliff and Susan, who were on the way to the sheriff's office.

All of them felt sick with horror when Ann and Dan had told their story. Cliff picked up the telephone.

"Who are you calling?" asked Dan.

"The state police," said Cliff, "and the mayor's office."

"Okay," said Ann. "We'll go get Jake while you make the calls. Would you also call John Ward and George Granger? Ask everybody to meet at the Proud house."

"I'll do that," said Susan.

Dan had driven away before Susan got the chance to say that neither John Ward nor George Granger answered the telephone.

It was full daylight when Dan pulled the car up near the red barn.

He and Ann got out and walked toward the back door. Jake never locked his door. He always said people were as welcome as they wanted to be. Dan opened the door and held it for Ann.

In the kitchen, Ann saw three men sitting around the table in the early morning light. There were Jake Fitzgibbon, John Ward, and George Granger.

The skin of their faces was frog green. Their

eyes turned toward her, popping from their heads. Their mouths were wide slits, smiling terrible smiles.

6

"Tell me everything you did yesterday," said Dr. Proud. "Tell me where you were. Tell me what you drank. Tell me what you ate."

Jake Fitzgibbon, John Ward, and George Granger sat in Dr. Proud's examining room. Cliff and Susan and old Jane Marsh were there too. Ann held small Jane on her lap. While Dr. Proud asked questions, Dan lit a fire. The spring morning was cold in the house by the sea.

"First," said Jake, "tell us what you think is the matter with us. Can you help us, Dr. Proud?" Jake's speech was a little thick. His tongue was too large in his mouth now.

"You have begun to take on a number of the physical characteristics of frogs," said Dr. Proud. "I want to find out how it happened. That's why I must ask some questions."

Each man told about his day. Jake had taken care of the animals and the fields of his farm. John Ward had worked at his bank. George Granger had seen to his guests at Blackstone. They had all eaten their usual food, had their usual drinks. The only thing they had done together was to meet for some early-morning fishing at Pine Pond.

Ann sat forward. Pine Pond! That was where Dr. Storm got his frogs. She spoke to small Jane, who was on her lap.

"Jane, were you near Pine Pond yesterday, or the day before?" asked Ann.

"The day before yesterday," said Jane. "I wanted to catch tadpoles for the tank in the third-grade room."

Jane stopped.

"What happened?" said Dan. He bent and took her hand gently. "It's important, Jane."

"Dr. Storm was there," said Jane. "You know, that fat man? He had a net with a long handle. He was catching frogs. He was nice. He let me watch. He even helped me catch four tadpoles.

29

But he held my hand too hard. Something in his hand hurt me."

Small Jane held up her right hand. On it was the same dark, ugly spot Ann and Dan had seen on the dead man's back.

"Look here," said Jake.

"And here," said John Ward and George Granger.

They all three held up their right hands.

"Dr. Storm was getting frogs when we were fishing," said Jake. "He shook our hands, too."

Dr. Proud and Dan examined the hands. "Burns," said Dr. Proud. "The kind of burns an acid makes."

Dad nodded. "There are poisons that burn slowly through the skin. Ann and I think Dr. Storm's formula works like that. If Dr. Storm held a piece of cotton or cloth soaked with the formula in a hand that was gloved—"

"He *was* wearing heavy rubber gloves," said George.

"He held my hand with his big black glove," said small Jane.

"That's it, then," said Ann. "We know how he gives the formula. What we don't know is why. And, most important, how to find an antidote."

"The antidote is most important," said Dr.

Proud. "Jane dear, take small Jane downstairs for some cake and milk."

Old Jane Marsh understood. She took her granddaughter from the room.

"The antidote is important," said Dr. Proud. "Jane's blood pressure is way up. If it goes much higher, it will cause a stroke—even death."

"Like the body on the beach," said Susan.

"Yes. I think the final cause of his death was a stroke," said Dr. Proud.

"Is there nothing you can do for us now?" said Jake quietly.

"Dr. Storm is an old friend," said Dr. Proud. "I shall tell him he must begin this morning on the antidote. In the meantime, I will give each of you medicine for pain. And—"

"And?" repeated John Ward.

"And remember that a frog's skin needs to be kept damp. Don't dry out. I will also give you something to keep your blood pressure down," said Dr. Proud.

Cliff had kept in the background. Now he spoke.

"I've called the state police," he said. "They are sending an officer and a doctor."

"Did you explain the problem?" said Ann.

"No," said Cliff. "No one would have believed

a word. All I said was we had bad trouble."

"What did you say the trouble was?" asked Ann.

"I called it an epidemic disease after you called me about Jake and John and George," said Cliff. There had been several talks.

"It is a disease at that," said Ann. "And the cause isn't a germ, but the mind of one man."

"And we'd better get that one man before he can shake any more hands," said Dan.

Ann stayed at the house to work with Uncle Charles. The others went off to find Dr. Storm.

For a few hours, things were quiet.

Then four people came to the Proud house. There were two fishermen, a teacher, and the boy who worked in the hardware store. They came one after the other, to be examined by Dr. Proud.

Their skins were green. Their mouths were slits. Their eyes had begun to pop. Their tongues were long and thick and sticky.

But not one of them had been near Dr. Emil Storm. No one had even seen him.

Ann had spent her life studying plants and animals. She wanted to protect them from harm. Now it was time to protect human life.

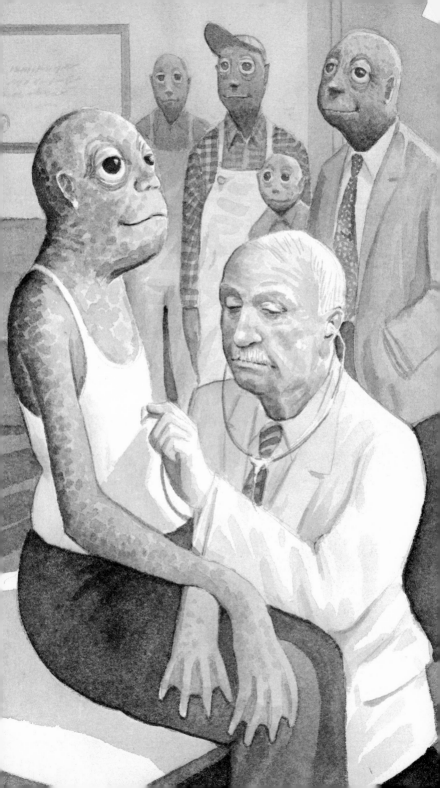

These four had been infected without being near Dr. Storm. That meant he had found another way to give his formula to people. How? thought Ann. In some sort of food? In a drink?

She looked out toward the sea. How far can he reach now? To the whole country? To the whole world?

Why? What turned a great scientist into a madman?

Maybe if she could understand him, she could stop him.

"Their blood pressure is not so high as the others'," said Uncle Charles quietly.

"He may have changed the formula," said Ann. "That would mean he wants people alive, not dead. But why turned into frogs, Uncle Charles? Why frogs?"

Ann needed some air. She went out back to feel the sea wind. Mary and Todd Dodge were down on the beach. They were running with their children. It was good to see the four healthy runners after so much horror and sickness.

She hated having to stop them. She hated having to warn them of the horror that had come to Proud Point.

34

7

An hour later, Dan called Ann.

"We looked everywhere," said Dan. "We went up to Pine Pond. We checked out every house. We even searched the high school. We warned everyone. At least everyone is ready for trouble now."

"Did you find Dr. Storm?" said Ann.

"We found him all right. He was sitting in his own lab. He was doing some tests. Ann, it was so odd to see him calm and cheerful. When he saw Jake's poor face, he nodded as if he'd been given a present."

"I'm on my way," said Ann.

"Of course, I don't want people to die," said Dr. Storm to Ann.

Ann had run up the beach and across the salt marshes. She had gotten to Blackstone's dark walls in under ten minutes.

"Then what do you want?" said Ann. Her bright eyes blazed. She was thinking of small Jane and all the others.

Dr. Storm came closer to Ann. He seemed eager to talk. He seemed to want to explain. He sat on a stool close to where Ann stood. Dan moved forward. He wanted to be near Ann in case Dr. Storm made any sudden move.

So far, the scientist seemed only to want to talk.

"What I want," he said, "is to help them."

"Help them!" said Ann. "Look at Jake!"

"Yes, help them. Yes, I look at Jake. And I am proud. I have studied the sea my whole life. And I have studied the history of the earth. I study also the future of our planet, as well as the past. And the longer I study, the more I see that the seas will return to flood the land as they did before."

Dr. Storm's round face lit up. His hands waved in the air.

"Can you see now what I am doing?" he said.

"All life began in the sea. All life will have to return to the sea when the land is flooded again. I must find a way for humans to live both on the land and in the sea. The body of the frog can do this. Our bodies must also be able to do this."

"What about our human brains, the human spirit?" asked Ann.

"My formula will save those. It must," said Dr. Storm. "Now do you see what I'm doing?"

"Yes, I see what you are doing," said Ann. "You are hurting and killing people, in the name of science."

"But you don't understand," said Emil Storm.

"She understands just fine," said Dan. "All we want from you now, Dr. Storm, is that you spend every waking hour finding an antidote."

Jake could hardly talk now. His words were thick and slow. But he tried. "Let me . . . live out . . . my own life. . . . Leave future . . . to God."

"We've sent for help," said Ann. "We'll take turns keeping you under guard, Dr. Storm. Just start looking for the antidote. And tell us how you've been spreading this thing, so we can stop it."

"Too late," said Dr. Storm. "When I realized it would take too long to touch everyone, I found

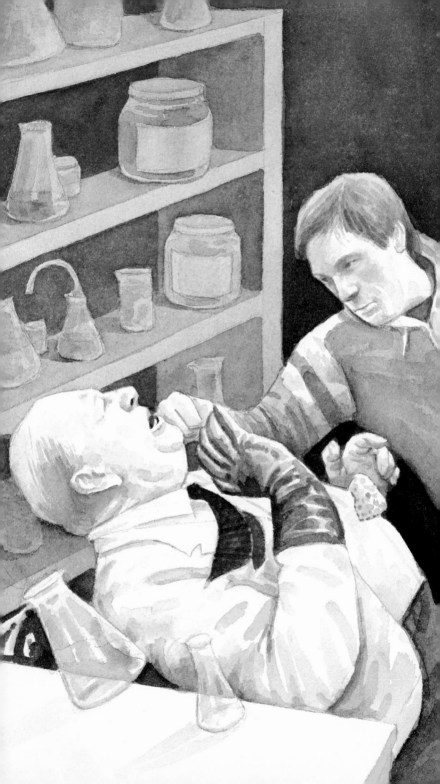

a better way. I made the formula into pills. The formula is now in the town water supply. I dropped the pills in several hours ago."

Dr. Storm stopped talking a moment.

"What I still don't understand is why some people change quickly and some change more slowly. I wonder how many will not change at all. I must ask you to excuse me. I must go back to my work now."

"You're *mad*," said Ann in horror.

The word seemed to anger Dr. Storm. He pulled on a glove. He grabbed a small sponge. He jumped at Ann.

But Dan was there first. He hit hard. The sponge did not strike Ann.

The sponge did touch Dr. Storm's bare left hand.

He would now need the antidote for himself.

8

Then they left Dr. Storm—working hard.

Dan telephoned Cliff. Everyone had to be warned about the water supply. Someone was sent to guard Dr. Storm. As they crossed the salt marshes, Jake's breath grew uneven.

"I . . . feel . . . weak," he said. "Dizzy . . . too. So many . . . changes . . . in my body."

Dan put an arm around his brother. "What about you two?" he asked John and George.

"My mind feels worse than my body," said John. "All I can think is that I've turned into a freak. All I want to do is hide."

"I feel the same way," said George. "And I'm

getting more like a freak every hour. Look at my hands."

George put out his hands for Ann to see in the clear noon light. They were now webbed between the fingers. The webbed green hands were already more frog-like than human.

"I'd rather die than look like this," said John. He had always been proud of his good looks, his fine clothes.

"No, you wouldn't," said George. "You come with me, John. The three of us will go to Jake's farm and wait it out together. Dan will let us know if there's any way we can help."

Ann stood there quietly. They were brave men. They faced a horrible death. Or, if they lived, an even more horrible life.

The three men went off.

Ann and Dan went to Cliff's office. He and Susan were waiting for the state police. Susan gave them sandwiches and coffee.

"I made the coffee from bottled water," said Cliff. "Everybody's using bottled water now."

Ann was glad just to sit.

"Now you two go in back and get a few hours' sleep," Susan said. "We'll need you when help gets here."

41

The police helicopter arrived at four in the afternoon. A state police officer, Sergeant Watson, got out. So did a medical examiner, a Dr. Adler.

Ann and Dan were waiting. So was everyone else.

"I hear you may have an epidemic. I'd like to meet Dr. Proud and see his patients first," said Dr. Adler.

Perfect, thought Ann. He'll see what's happened right away. He'll get the right labs working on this.

They went to the Proud house. They saw small Jane. She lay on Ann's bed. Her green skin, her frog-like face looked terrible. And her hands had begun to web like George's, like the hands of the dead man.

They saw the two fishermen, the teacher, the boy who worked at the hardware store. They drove out and saw Jake, George, and John.

On the way back, Ann told Dr. Adler and Sergeant Watson all about Dr. Storm and what he had done.

"You can see Proud Point is in real trouble," said Ann.

"Yes," said Dr. Adler. "You've got a bad epidemic here."

"Epidemic!" said Ann. "Did you hear what I've been saying? We don't have an epidemic, Dr. Adler. We have a madman."

"Your Uncle Charles told me all about Dr. Storm while we were in the other room with the little girl," said Dr. Adler. "Just an old man who's no use to anyone anymore. Your uncle says he tells a lot of wild tales."

"Now listen here," said Dan. He stopped the car. "Ann is telling the truth. You've got to listen. You've got to help these people. Get them to a good hospital. Get good scientists to work on an antidote to Dr. Storm's formula."

"Dr. Proud can take care of Proud Point's epidemic. He told me himself it was just a disease. And that he's got enough medicine. Now keep driving, young man. My helicopter is waiting."

"And no one is to leave town," said the officer. "Right, Dr. Adler?"

"No one," said Dr. Adler. "We don't want this thing to spread."

They watched the helicopter disappear.

Ann said, "I don't believe what he said about Uncle Charles, Dan. Something must be wrong."

Dan put an arm around her. "Of course

there's something wrong. And the worst of it is, we're on our own."

"Not exactly," said Ann. She put an arm around him, too.

"Dan, we have to check up on Uncle Charles," said Ann.

"We're worried about what he told Dr. Adler. Uncle Charles even said he has the medicine to cure everyone," Dan explained.

Susan put an arm around Ann. "And then you'll rest? This nightmare isn't going to change much in a few hours."

"Susan is right," said Dan. "We'll take some time off. This nightmare is not going to change much before morning."

But it did change. It got worse.

Ann and Dan found Uncle Charles in back of the house. He was standing on the high cliff. He was looking out to sea. The last of the fishing boats were coming in. Gulls flew high above them.

Ann put a hand on Dan's arm. Something was wrong. For one more moment, she didn't want to face it. She had loved Uncle Charles since she was a little girl.

Dan understood and waited.

Then the old doctor turned. Their last hope of medical help in Proud Point was gone.

Uncle Charles had the flat green head, the popping eyes, the slit mouth, and the webbed hands of the frog people. But something more had happened to him.

He did not look at them. He moved slowly toward a large, flat rock and gave a little jump. In a moment, he was squatting on it.

A small figure hopped past Ann just then. It had to be small Jane. Ann could hardly tell anymore. She was a little, bent-over figure. Her feet and hands were completely webbed. Her size was human. The shapes of her arms and legs were human. She still wore a human dress. Nothing else was left of the child Ann had known.

Jane hopped toward the figure on the rock. Ann watched as Uncle Charles and small Jane squatted side by side. They put out their tongues like frogs to catch any insect that passed too close.

Ann tried. So did Dan.

"Hello," they both called softly.

There was no answer.

They came closer.

The two frog people drew back.

46

"Dr. Storm has failed," said Ann. "When they don't die, they lose their minds."

"The very thing he wanted to save, the human mind and spirit, is gone," said Dan.

For tonight, there was nothing more they could do.

They went inland. Ann wanted to walk in the spring woods. She felt safer under the pine trees, away from the sea.

They sat on deep pine needles near a waterfall. There was an owl. Whippoorwills filled the night. And there was the sound of the wind in the trees.

At last Ann fell asleep in Dan's arms. He listened for a long time. But the frogs were silent that night.

Finally, he slept too.

9

Proud Point was full of frog people. Their eyes were popped wide. Their skin was green. Their mouths were slits. They had webbed hands and feet. Some had flat, hairless heads. Some hopped on frog-like legs.

They did not speak or smile. They didn't seem to hear. And they all behaved in the same mindless way.

John Ward kept on going to the bank. But he no longer cared about "big deals."

George Granger kept on finding strays. He brought more baby animals back to Blackstone than ever. It was as if his own sadness filled him with even more pity.

Jane Marsh went on running her store. Sometimes she couldn't remember the prices. Mostly, people paid what they wanted. Sometimes they paid nothing. Jane Marsh didn't care. Her mind, too, had gone with her human body.

Mike's Bar and Grill stayed open round the clock. Day or night, Mike never locked up. Drinkers went in. They took what they wanted, then went out.

Many people could still take care of their homes. Many could still take out the fishing boats. Some of the farmers brought in their crops and fed their chickens and milked their cows.

But there were the others. Others just hopped around town. They didn't talk anymore. Their long, sticky tongues made it hard to talk now.

One day, Ann noticed something new. Some of the frog people had stopped eating food. She and Dan had gone out to see Jake. Jake just sat at his kitchen table. His eyes stared at nothing. He pushed away the food Ann tried to give him.

Uncle Charles pushed food away, too. He didn't even come into the kitchen. He spent hours squatting out back on the large, flat rock. He ate only the flies he caught.

"They must be hungry," said Dan. "Their bodies need real food."

"Hungry and in pain," said Ann. "Look at Uncle Charles. The changes must be hurting him terribly."

Ann called the ones who ate flies the Second Stage people. Those who still ate human food were the First Stage people.

"Dan," she said, "why is it that some people haven't changed at all? If only we knew that! It might help in finding an antidote."

So far, about ten adults and four of Proud Point's children had not changed. They all met every day in Cliff's office. Work had to be planned. Food for the First Stage people had to be planned. Proud Point was still a town. Its people were still alive. They needed care.

And those ten survivors needed each other's hope.

There was no hope of help from Dr. Emil Storm. He was pop-eyed and frog green. He hopped around his lab. Notes lay on the floor. Test tubes were smashed.

No one could come to Proud Point to give

help. No one could leave to get help. All the roads were blocked by police cars. Helicopters watched the sea and woods.

Radio and television told people to stay away. "The town of Proud Point has an epidemic," said the news. "No one can enter or leave until the disease is under control."

Cliff called Dr. Adler. No help there.

All Ann and Dan and Cliff and Susan and the other survivors could do was wait and hope.

But they went on waiting.

By the end of the second week, the frog people changed again. They began to disappear.

10

Ann and Dan, Cliff and Susan now slept on cots in Cliff's office. They took turns taking care of problems. They also watched television, listened to the radio.

One morning, Ann went home. She needed clean clothes.

The Proud house was a mess.

"Uncle Charles?" Ann called.

She looked for her uncle in one room after another. All she saw were overturned tables, broken lamps, broken chairs.

She found her uncle finally. He was on his own bedroom balcony. The frog face stuck out of his old blue shirt. The webbed hands waved at Ann one moment. Then he gave a quick jump past her. He was downstairs and out the front door a moment later.

Ann ran after him. He went down Center Street, along the rock path, toward the dunes. Then he suddenly turned into the woods.

Ann was a runner. Even she had trouble keeping up with a man who could jump like a frog on long human legs. But she kept behind him until they got to Pine Pond.

He sat down on a flat rock at the edge of the pond. Every few moments, his long, thick, sticky tongue shot out of his mouth. Every few moments, it brought back a fly or a bug.

As Ann looked around, she saw the others. She saw the rest of the frog people who had disappeared. They were doing exactly the same thing as Uncle Charles. They were feeding themselves. They came to Pine Pond to keep themselves alive on bugs.

Ann went back to town. She examined a piece of small Jane's skin under a microscope. They kept small Jane with them in Cliff's office. Small Jane didn't mind being cut. She didn't mind anything much anymore.

"Look at these, Dan, please," Ann said.

Dan looked at the slides Ann showed him.

"This one is Jane's skin," said Ann. She pointed to a slide.

"It looks most like this slide." Dan pointed to the first of the slides.

Ann nodded. "Exactly alike," said Ann. "Her skin is now exactly like that of a frog. The cells have changed completely."

Ann went into the bathroom just off the front office. Dan followed her. They both stared sadly at the little girl. Jane's poor green body stayed mostly under water now, in the tub. Her skin, like that of any frog, needed to be kept moist.

"The same question keeps coming over and over again into my mind," said Ann. "Why some of us and not others? We all had the same water."

Dan put an arm around her and led her back to the office. They made coffee. They sat down to talk it out all over again. "That's the most important question," said Dan. "Why some and not others? There has to be some natural antidote. If only we can find it before they die."

"Or live—which may be worse," said Ann softly. "So many are in such pain."

"The kids get to me the most," said Dan.

Ann took his hand. "I never realized how much I loved our peaceful life. Our teaching. Our running."

"Let's go for a run now," said Dan. "We can use the exercise. And running can ease the heartache—for a while."

The ten adults and four children met later as usual. As usual, Ann took skin and blood samples.

"I wish I knew more," said Ann. "I wish I could find something special about us. If there were something special, we could try to make a serum to help the others."

Dan looked around Cliff's office at the group. Mary and Todd Dodge owned the farm next to Jake's. They were a hard-working young couple. They and their two children were still okay.

Simon Jones was not hard-working. He was lazy. He borrowed more things than he returned. Even his running shoes were borrowed. He wore the same size as Dan.

Then there were Larry, Lily, and Honor Hart. The man and his two sisters had Proud Point's only book store.

And there were the two Browning children.

They sometimes did errands for the Harts or worked in their store. They read a lot of books. And they were on Dan's running team.

Cliff watched Dan look at the group.

"What special thing do they all have?" asked Cliff.

"Nothing that I can find in their blood or skin," said Ann.

"Nothing in the way they live and act," said Susan.

"How true," said Mary Dodge. She looked at her own fingernails. They were broken with field work. She looked at Honor Hart's fingernails. They were perfect pink ovals.

"You know it," said Simon Jones. He was once again eating more than his share of beans at dinner.

Ann sighed. "I'm used to observing animals. Sometimes people don't make much sense to me."

"That's the first thing to know about people," said Dan. "They don't make much sense. Mostly, they don't love right, or live right, or sleep right, or eat right, or exercise—" Dan stopped.

He rubbed his right knee. Ten or fifteen miles always set it to hurting.

Then his eyes gleamed.

"Something?" said Ann. She leaned toward him.

"Something," said Dan. "I can't think what took me so long."

He stood up, lifted his foot. He pointed to his tan and orange running shoes. "We're runners," he said. "All of us are runners. Whatever else is different among us, from Simon to the Dodges to the Harts to Cliff, Susan, you, me, even the four kids—every one of us is a long-distance runner."

Ann's eyes brightened too. "Body chemistry," she said. "The body chemistry of a runner changes. It takes up more oxygen. Other things, too. Those changes must protect us somehow."

An hour later, poor small Jane was dead. Her heart just stopped. Tears raced down Ann's cheeks. She packed a knapsack with notes and slides. She placed small Jane's body gently in a duffel bag to hide its form.

"We know something now," said Ann. "And she, poor little thing, is evidence. I'm going to New York for help."

No one argued. As a scientist, Ann could be of the most use.

But two absences couldn't be covered. The state police now checked the few people in Proud Point every day.

At dark, Dan helped Ann through the woods. There was a path past Pine Pond. After that there were thick trees and thick, thick brambles. But Dan and Ann had grown up walking in these woods. They knew how to get through. Sometimes they went on hands and knees. But they got through.

"If this weren't so awful, it would be fun," said Ann.

"I like your kind of mind," said Dan. "It's so clear."

They needed to joke. They had come to the end of the woods. The police cordon was out there.

Dan went out alone. He wanted their attention.

"I'd like to visit some friends in the next town," he said to one of the officers.

"You know you can't pass," said the officer.

Some of the policemen backed away from him.

They are afraid to catch the disease, thought Dan. Good.

He walked among the police, talking. They were all watching him closely.

He kept talking. "Just for a few hours. I'm really tired of being in one place so much," said Dan. He made sure he sounded as if he didn't

know the rules very well. So he could keep arguing with them. And they had to go on watching him closely.

After ten minutes, Dan knew Ann was safe. They had planned for her to creep along the dark edge of the highway for about a mile. After that, she was on her own.

"You'll really have to go back to Proud Point now," said the first officer to Dan.

Dan seemed to give in. "Okay," he said.

He turned back into the woods.

Ann was gone.

11

Ann sat on a stool in a lab. Her friend, Dr. Mary Stevens, examined small Jane. Dr. Stevens gave careful attention to the skin. She gave no attention to Ann's story about Dr. Storm.

"The disease is what matters," she said. "It may have come from a madman's pills. But the madman isn't the point. Finding the antidote is. I'm going to call a friend in Washington. He's a biochemist—one of the best. I want him to see your notes, slides, your data about the runners."

"Will you tell him about Dr. Storm's experiments?" Ann tried one more time to interest her in the madman. "What if other scientists are doing the same thing in other towns, other cities, other countries?"

"Are you talking about a world plot?" Mary Stevens smiled at her friend. "That sounds like a bad movie."

Dr. Stevens turned back to small Jane's body. "Poor little thing," she said. "We'll find a cure for the others. Don't worry."

"What are you going to tell the biochemist?" Ann asked.

"That we have found a new disease. That it causes frog characteristics. That it spreads. That it can kill. A new fatal disease will get top attention. Whatever causes it."

"Can Proud Point be opened up again?" asked Ann.

"No," said the doctor. "Maybe Storm's pills cause the disease, as you say. But maybe it is catching in other ways. We can't let Proud Point's Frog Disease spread if we can help it."

Now it had a name. Proud Point's Frog Disease.

Ann went home. She hitched a ride as she had before. She phoned Dan to signal that she was near. He went to the police cordon again.

And again Ann got past them.

12

At Proud Point, things were worse than they were before.

Ann had only been away two days. But the town was nearly empty now. A few frog people hopped in the streets. Some were at Pine Pond. Many were on the beach. They stayed half in, half out of the water.

"Frogs can't live in salt water," said Ann. "But the frog people can. Dr. Storm really did plan for us to return to the sea."

"He also planned for our minds and hearts and spirits to remain human," said Dan. "Remember? Look at those poor creatures."

Ann and Dan were standing high on the dunes. It was a dark night. The ragged moon shed only a pale light. They could see the frog-like bodies creeping darkly on the sand below.

In different parts of town, the survivors were keeping watch. Changes had been happening so fast that Ann felt there was going to be a final stage. She felt it could happen soon.

"Look," said Ann. She pointed her flashlight up the beach in the direction of Blackstone.

A round, short, frog-like figure came out of the salt marshes. It hopped and crawled onto the beach. It pulled itself into the middle of the group.

For the first time, there was sound.

Ann heard the sound. She wondered why she had never noticed its absence before.

The sound was the sound of croaking. For the first time, it was there. This leader—and leader it seemed to be—this figure in the middle of all the others sent out the sound. And the sound came back from all around. It came from the woods. It came from the town. It came from all along the beach.

There was a movement from every direction. Tens of the frog-like creatures, twenties of them, nearly two hundred began to gather. They

gathered around the leader, croaking in answer to his call.

Then Ann gasped. She suddenly knew what was to happen. As she and Dan watched, it did happen.

The leader made a sudden motion. He led them away—away from the beach, straight into the sea.

Susan and Cliff and the other survivors came running up to the dunes. They, too, had heard the croaking. As they stood there, all the frog people disappeared into the waves.

"The leader was Dr. Storm," said Ann. "Has he led them to death? To another life? Will we ever know?"

13

So many people they loved were gone. Just gone.

Ann cried softly. Dan held her close.

"They were in such pain," said Ann. "I guess anything is better than that."

The survivors went back to the sheriff's office. Cliff made a lot of coffee.

"We have to think about getting away from Proud Point," said Dan.

"Yes," said Susan. "We've got to get away from this horror."

"Not just that," said Cliff. "Dan and I have been talking. We still don't know all there is to know about the water supply. It may still have Dr. Storm's formula in it. And we can't live on bottled water forever."

"True," said Ann. "We still don't have an antidote. We just think that something in our bodies caused by running has saved us. So far. And even that could change."

"The children must go," said Honor Hart. "But I've lived in Proud Point all my life. I wouldn't want to go anywhere else."

Larry and Lily felt the same.

So did Simon Jones.

Jim Dodge said, "We've talked it over. The other kids and me, I mean. We want to stay. Mother and Dad agree."

Mary Dodge nodded. "We'll take all four children to our farm. We'll keep them running. We'll give them milk to drink. We'll wait and see."

"Miss Derry," said Jim. "Do you think Dr. Storm was right? Do you think we all might have to go back into the sea someday?"

"It's always possible," said Ann. "Someday."

"Then doesn't a scientist like Dr. Storm have to make experiments to help us? To change us so we can? Live in the sea, I mean?" said Jim.

"Yes, of course, scientists must make experiments. We must understand the planet we live on. We do have to learn to handle the future. But not at the expense of sensitive, living creatures," said Ann.

She thought of Jake, of Uncle Charles, of George Granger and John Ward, of old Jane Marsh—of all the people out there in the sea. Only God knew if their minds were still sensitive to the nightmare they were living through!

14

The state police still kept Proud Point cut off.

Dr. Stevens got a telephone call through to Ann. The biochemist in Washington had put out an alarm. The President of the United States declared the Frog Disease to be a national problem. The Department of Health called the Frog Disease a national emergency. The race against more deaths was on. The cure had to be found before more people became frog people.

Ann had needed some quiet. She and Dan followed the events on the television set in the old Proud sea cliff house. Against the pounding of the sea on the rocks below, they listened in horror.

There were reports from Japan, England, Moscow, Paris, Peking, Africa. The frog pills were everywhere. The Frog Disease was everywhere. Spread by Dr. Storm? By many Dr. Storms?

Scientists in every country worked around the clock. The world waited and hoped. Hoped that time wouldn't run out. Hoped that enough people would be left to keep on working.

Runners everywhere checked in to hospitals, in to laboratories. They were needed for testing. People who hadn't run before were urged to do so now.

Then, for many days, the news about the Frog Disease dropped off. Ann and Dan heard fewer reports. The radio and television programs were more normal again.

Ann began to relax a little. Dan began to think they could go out and run and swim and enjoy the coming summer a little.

The good news came at last. An announcer said a cure had been found. Ann sat with Dan in front of the television set. The whole story was told again, about Proud Point, about the begin-

ning of the Frog Disease, about how Dr. Mary Stevens worked with scientists in Washington until they found the cure. People in every country from Japan to Russia to England to Africa were now following this cure.

Ann felt her breath come a lot easier. She poured tea for Dan and they smiled at one another as the program went on.

"It's a simple cure," said the reporter. "Now that you all know it is far better to do as Dr. Storm says, the cure for still being human is easy."

What followed was a list of numbers to call for the pills.

Then the announcer came back on the screen. He croaked the numbers aloud through a slit mouth.

Then the screen went dead.